13

5

*To Caroline for her enthusiasm
and encouragement.*

SPLASH!
A RED FOX BOOK 0 09 944797 5

First published in Great Britain by Hutchinson,
an imprint of Random House Children's Books

Hutchinson edition published 2003
Red Fox edition published 2004

1 3 5 7 9 10 8 6 4 2

Red Fox Books are published by Random House Children's Books,
61– 63 Uxbridge Road, London W5 5SA,
a division of The Random House Group Ltd,
in Australia by Random House Australia (Pty) Ltd,
20 Alfred Street, Milsons Point, Sydney, NSW 2061, Australia,
in New Zealand by Random House New Zealand Ltd,
18 Poland Road, Glenfield, Auckland 10, New Zealand,
and in South Africa by Random House (Pty) Ltd,
Endulini, 5A Jubilee Road, Parktown 2193, South Africa

THE RANDOM HOUSE GROUP Limited Reg. No. 954009
www.kidsatrandomhouse.co.uk

A CIP catalogue record for this book is available from the British Library.

Printed in Hong Kong

Splash!

Jane Hissey

RED FOX

Old Bear and the other toys were having a lovely day at the sea-side. Little Bear had never seen the sea before.

"It's bigger than the biggest bath," he cried as he chased his new beach ball in and out of the waves, "and I'll never run out of sand, even if I build a hundred sandcastles."

Little Bear left his beach ball and began to dig
with his spade. Rabbit soon joined him.

"What are we making?" asked Rabbit from
the bottom of the hole.

"Well it was meant to be a sandcastle,"
said Little Bear, "but it seems to be
going *down* instead of *up*."

"It could be a boat,"
said Sailor."

They patted down
the sides of the hole and
found a plank of wood to make a seat.
Jolly Tall fetched a long piece of driftwood for a mast.

"What a lovely boat," said
Bramwell Brown as he brought
them his red towel to use as a sail.

"And it really moves," said Little Bear.

"It can't *really move*," said Duck.
"It's made of sand."

"Well it's much nearer the sea than
when we started," said Little Bear.

"It's not the boat that's moved,"
explained Sailor. "It's the sea. The
tide has come in. It goes in and out
every day to wash the beach clean."

Little Bear suddenly remembered his new ball
and ran to where he'd left it by the water.
"Oh no," he cried, "the sea has taken my ball."
Before anyone could stop him, he had jumped into
his bucket and was heading out to sea.

"Come back!" shouted Old Bear. "You can't go to sea in a bucket!"
"It's all right," called Little Bear, "I'll be back in a minute."

The bucket bobbed up and down in the waves and Little Bear bounced about inside it. He began to think that this wasn't such a good idea after all.

He couldn't see the lost ball anywhere. Perhaps a shark has eaten it, he thought, and then he began to worry that a shark might eat him too.

"I'm coming back!" he called, but when he tried to paddle, he just went round and round in circles.

Old Bear was right, thought Little Bear, you can't go to sea in a bucket.

Suddenly there was a big gust of wind. The bucket wobbled wildly from side to side then tipped right over. With a splash Little Bear tumbled into the sea and the bucket slowly sank beneath the waves.

"Help!" gasped Little Bear, clinging to his spade to stay afloat. "Somebody help!"

"Hold on, Little Bear," called Sailor from the beach, "we'll throw you a rope."

But, at that moment, they saw a
fluffy, white face pop out of the
water right in front of Little Bear.
It was a small, furry creature
wearing a string of sea-shells round
its neck and his bucket on its head!

"I believe this is yours," it said to
Little Bear.

"My bucket!" spluttered Little Bear.
"Thank you. But . . . but who are you?
Are you a shark?"

"Not a *shark*," laughed the creature. "I'm a
seal. My name is Splash. Now, quickly, climb on
my back. We don't want you to sink like your bucket!"

Little Bear scrambled on to Splash's back and waved triumphantly
to the others. They cheered when they saw that he was safe.
"What were you doing so far from the beach?" asked Splash.

"It was the wind's fault," explained Little Bear. "It blew me out of my bucket."

"But you can't go to sea in a bucket," said Splash.

"I know that *now*," said Little Bear and he explained how his new beach ball had been taken away by the tide.

"I'll probably *never* find it," he said sadly.

"I think I know where your ball is," said Splash. "I'll show you."

With Little Bear clinging to her sea-shell
necklace Splash swam swiftly through the waves.
 "This is like a speed boat!" cried Little Bear.
"We're going faster than the wind."
 They soon arrived at a rocky ledge and
before Little Bear knew what was happening,
they had slipped through a curtain of
sea-weed and into a secret cave.

Little Bear stared in amazement.
All around them were rows and rows of
sea-side things: sandals and spades, towels and toys,
buckets, balls and boats.

"It's a treasure cave," gasped Little Bear, "and there's
my ball. How did it get in here?"

"I rescued it," said Splash. "I found all these things
floating in the sea. The tide takes them from the beach
so I save them and bring them here."

Splash hopped over to Little Bear's ball and bounced it down to where he was waiting.

"Oh thank you," cried Little Bear. "But what will you do with all the other things?"

"I play with them for a little while," explained Splash, "then when nobody's looking, I take them back to the beach."

"But aren't you sorry not to have them any more?" asked Little Bear, balancing a pair of sunglasses on his nose and a straw hat on his head.

"Not really," laughed Splash. "There are always more lost things to be rescued!"

"I'd like to stay here for ever," said Little Bear,
"it's like a toy shop."
　"But your friends will be worried about you,"
said Splash. "I think I should take you
back to the beach."
　Clutching his things, Little Bear
climbed onto Splash's back.
Then together they slipped
through the sea-weed
curtain, and set off
for the shore.

Old Bear and the other toys were waiting anxiously on the beach. Little Bear couldn't wait to introduce his new friend.

"Thank you, Splash," said Bramwell. "You saved Little Bear."

"It was a pleasure," said Splash. "And it's been fun having someone new to play with."

"You must see Splash's treasure cave," said Little Bear, "it's amazing."

"Another time perhaps," said Old Bear. "It's getting late and we really should be going home."

"Can Splash come and live with us?" cried Little Bear. "I could make her a cave under my bed and she could swim in the bath." "It does sound fun," said Old Bear, "but Splash already has a home; she lives here, by the sea."

"And who would return
all the lost things if I weren't here?"
laughed Splash. "But," she added kindly,
"I have something you *can* take home with you, Little Bear."

She took off her shell necklace and slipped it over Little Bear's head. "There," she said. "You can remember our sea-side adventure every time you wear this. And come back soon, won't you?"

"Oh thank you, Splash!" cried Little Bear. "I will!"